A peach tree grew in the old alley where Xiaoke's dad had lived as a child. Xiaoke's dad had planted the peach pit himself, and it had grown into a big tree. Xiaoke loved this peach tree. He thought of the tree as his brother—his peach tree brother.

Xiaoke's grandparents had passed away, but his dad still missed his old home. So he and Xiaoke visited the neighborhood on Chinese New Year's Eve. There they pasted a red spring poem on the door of the old house.

"WELCOME SPRING.
WELCOME GOOD LUCK.
GOOD FORTUNE IS COMING!"

They returned on the second day of the next month. All the barbershops in the old neighborhood were crowded with people wanting new hairstyles to welcome spring.

"ON THE SECOND DAY OF THE SECOND MONTH, THE DRAGON RAISES ITS HEAD.

A HAIRCUT ON THAT DAY MAKES US SPIRITED ALL THE YEAR AHEAD."

The barber's scissors nibbled away at people's thick hair like a feasting silkworm.

But Xiaoke didn't want a haircut.

When his dad wasn't looking, Xiaoke snuck out of the barbershop and returned to the old alley. He wanted to see his peach tree brother.

The run-down houses all had "Chai" painted on them, which meant they were marked for demolition. Some of them had already collapsed.

The spring poems pasted
on Chinese New Year's
Eve had been blown
off the doors. They flew
through the alley like
winged red ribbons.

The alley was dark
and deserted, with
not a soul in sight.

Everyone had moved away.

Xiaoke's peach tree brother stood alone.

Its only company was a small puppy.

With the old alley facing demolition, the peach tree brother bowed its head. It had nowhere to go. Cold wind rushed by, rustling the peach tree's leaves. It seemed to be weeping. Leaning against his brother, Xiaoke didn't know what to say.

The boy took off his long scarf and wrapped
it around the trunk, soothing the tree.

Suddenly, a heavy machine appeared. Xiaoke stood between it and the tree.

"Don't knock down the tree!" Xiaoke cried. "It's my brother."

"You don't look like him," said the driver.

At once, Xiaoke stood upright like the tree.

"The peach tree's hair is neat, but yours is so messy," the driver said, pointing to the tree's canopy.

"Wait a minute, please," Xiaoke begged the driver.

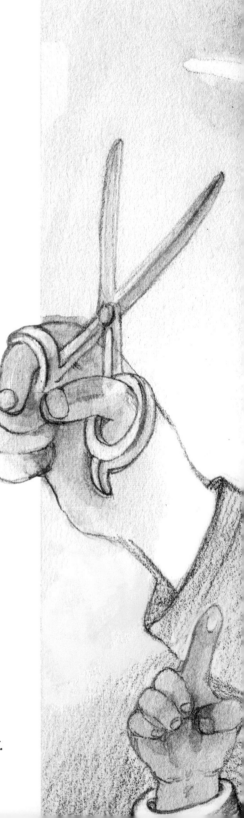

Xiaoke rushed back to the barbershop. Dipping his finger in some water, he drew a peach tree's canopy on the barber's mirror. He asked the barber to give him a hairstyle like the tree's.

Xiaoke rushed back to the peach tree and
stood next to it, showing off his new hairstyle.

The driver paused for a moment. Then he gave
a thumbs-up and moved his machine aside.

"Move the tree as soon as
possible," the driver said.
"It'll die if it stays here."

So Xiaoke and his dad dug up the
peach tree. They transplanted it in
the yard of their apartment building.

With the arrival of the peach tree, the
entire neighborhood seemed brighter.

Xiaoke was convinced his peach tree
brother would take root and sprout again.

He watered it faithfully. He
even let the puppy, who had
followed him home, pee on
the tree to add nutrients.

Soon spring came. The peach tree sprouted new leaves and flowers. Xiaoke realized that the old saying was true. He and his peach tree brother had been blessed by a haircut on the second day of the second month.

WELCOME SPRING.
WELCOME GOOD LUCK.

GOOD FORTUNE HAS COME!

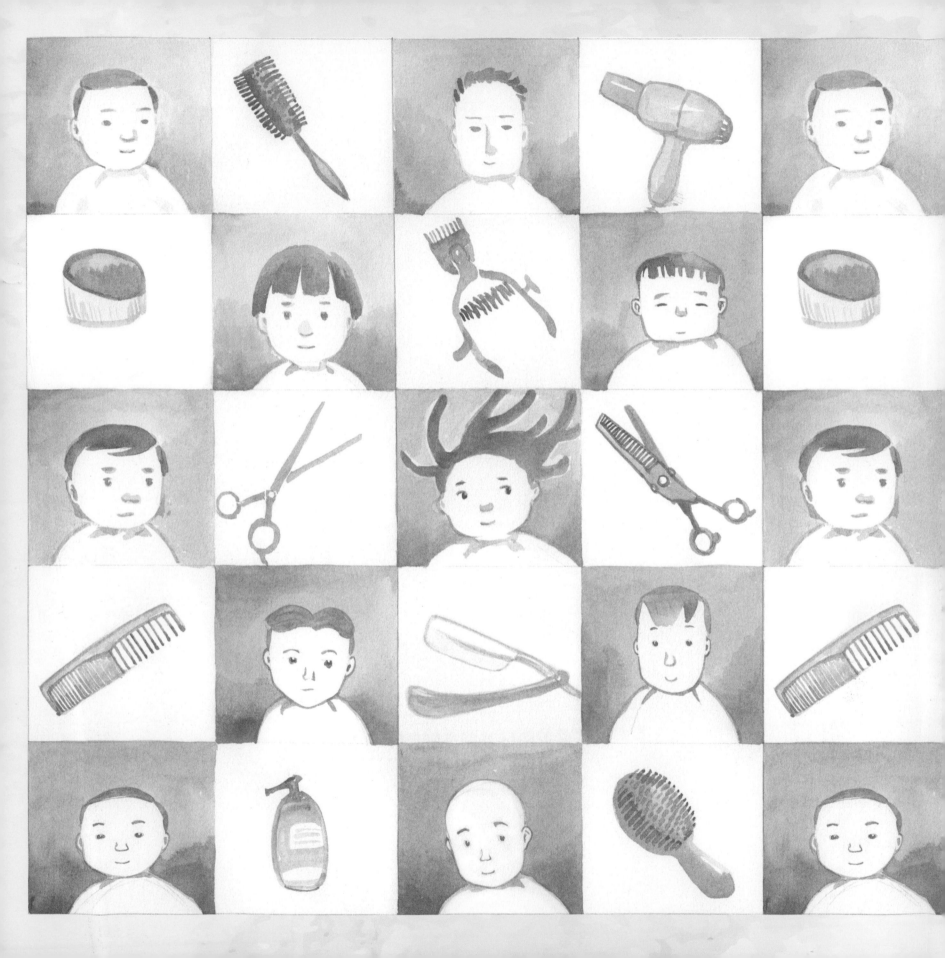